Little, Brown and Company

Hachette Book Group
237 Park Avenue, New York, NY 10017
Visit our website at www.lb-kids.com

Little, Brown and Company is a division of Hachette Book Group, Inc.
The Little, Brown name and logo are trademarks of Hachette Book Group, Inc.

The publisher is not responsible for websites (or their content)
that are not owned by the publisher.

First Edition: September 2013

ISBN 978-0-316-18866-1

10 9 8 7 6 5 4 3

Library of Congress Control Number: 2013939489

CW

Printed in the United States of America

LICENSED BY:

TRANSFORMERS PRIME
BEAST HUNTERS

OPTIMUS PRIME VERSUS PREDAKING

Adapted by John Sazaklis
Based on the episode "Evolution"
written by Steven Melching

LITTLE, BROWN AND COMPANY
New York Boston

Deep in a cavern lies a secret laboratory. Megatron and his minions enter to check on their latest project. The Decepticons are using Synthetic Energon to clone an army of Predacons, a long-lost race of beast warriors.

"What is your status, Shockwave?" Megatron asks the lead scientist.

"The process is almost complete, my lord," he replies.

Megatron is pleased. "Soon I will lead them in annihilating the Autobots!"

All of a sudden, a monstrous roar echoes through the lab. A dragon appears and changes form.

"I am Predaking!" he bellows. "And *I* will lead this army!"

Meanwhile, at the Autobots' base, Optimus Prime and his team are monitoring all quadrants.

"Decepticon activity is at a lull," Optimus Prime reports. "I fear that Megatron is planning something big."

Just then, an alarm blares.

"Optimus!" Ratchet cries. "Our scanners are detecting exposed Energon!"

"Activate the GroundBridge," the leader commands. "With our reserves at such a critical low, we must investigate." Then Optimus turns to the rest of his team and says, "Autobots, roll out!"

Team Prime tracks the Energon to a rocky mountainside. From a distance, they see Decepticon troopers exiting a cave pushing mine carts loaded with the life-giving element.

"Look at all that sweet fuel!" exclaims Smokescreen.

"They are harvesting the power source," Arcee says.

Optimus Prime drops down in front of the troopers. "Decepticons, step away from the Energon and surrender," he says.

The troopers do not comply. Instead, they attack. Optimus returns fire. The Decepticons fall at his feet, but others take their places. Optimus Prime is outnumbered!

In a flash, the troopers are blasted backward. Optimus turns to see Bulkhead, Bumblebee, and Ultra Magnus leap down from a ridge. They rush to the rescue with their weapons blazing.

As another wave of Decepticons approaches, Bumblebee, Arcee, and Ultra Magnus charge from behind the trees. The new troopers are caught in the crossfire and taken down quickly. Only Team Prime is left standing.

"Thank you, my friends," Optimus says.

Ultra Magnus and Wheeljack volunteer to explore the cave. They walk down a long tunnel leading into the Decepticon lab. The Autobots react in horror at the sight within—rows and rows of cloning tanks full of Predacons! "Well, this is a whole lot of ugly," jokes Wheeljack.

Shockwave appears from behind a table and flips a switch. The generator connected to the Predacon pods sparks. Before the Autobots can raise their weapons, the evil scientist changes into a tank and fires his cannon.

The Autobots dive for cover as Shockwave escapes to warn Predaking about their presence.

"Let's get him!" Wheeljack shouts, but Ultra Magnus stops him.

"Act swiftly or we won't stand a chance against this many monsters," he says, pointing to the pods. "Blast these beasts back to the Rust Age!"

"Yes, sir," Wheeljack replies, and launches a grenade. "Hit the deck!"

The heroes shield themselves as the explosion destroys the Predacons.

When the smoke clears, a furious Predaking emerges.

"What have you done to my brethren?" he yells. "I will avenge my army!"

Fueled with rage, Predaking charges at the Autobots.

"Let's dance!" Wheeljack shouts, and unsheathes his swords. Sparks fly as he slashes Predaking with the blades. Ultra Magnus hefts his mighty forge hammer and bashes the beast-bot. Predaking staggers but is unscathed.

"Prepare to perish!" Predaking shouts, countering with a barrage of blows. He pounds Wheeljack and Ultra Magnus into the ground. Towering over them, the Predacon unfurls his talons for the final strike.

Suddenly, a missile blasts Predaking into the cavern wall. Another figure enters the fray—Optimus Prime!

"How dare you!" Predaking growls. He leaps at the Autobot leader with a fierce intensity. "You will suffer most of all!"

"That remains to be seen," Optimus replies, catching Predaking's fist. The two bots battle, but they are evenly matched.

Predaking pushes his opponent up against the wall, digging his talons into Optimus's shoulders. The Autobot musters all his strength and throws a mighty uppercut that knocks the Predacon onto his back.

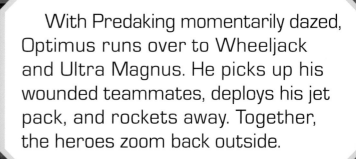

With Predaking momentarily dazed, Optimus runs over to Wheeljack and Ultra Magnus. He picks up his wounded teammates, deploys his jet pack, and rockets away. Together, the heroes zoom back outside.

Predaking recovers and switches into beast mode. The dragon flies out of the cavern. Optimus Prime weaves through the air.

"Prepare the GroundBridge!" Optimus commands. "NOW!"

Predaking spews a huge fireball at Team Prime. Seconds before impact, the Autobots disappear into the portal, which closes behind them.

The beast-bot is stranded on the mountainside. "This is not the end!" he roars. "I will have my revenge!"

Back at the base, the wounded Autobots receive medical attention. "Ratchet will take good care of you," Optimus says to Ultra Magnus.

"What happens when Predaking returns?" Ratchet asks.

"He doesn't stand a chance against us," Wheeljack answers, looking at his friends. "As long as we've got each other, we can face anything!"